VISIT AMAZON.COM FOR MORE
LITTLE HEDGEHOG BOOKS

MY NANA
LOVES ME

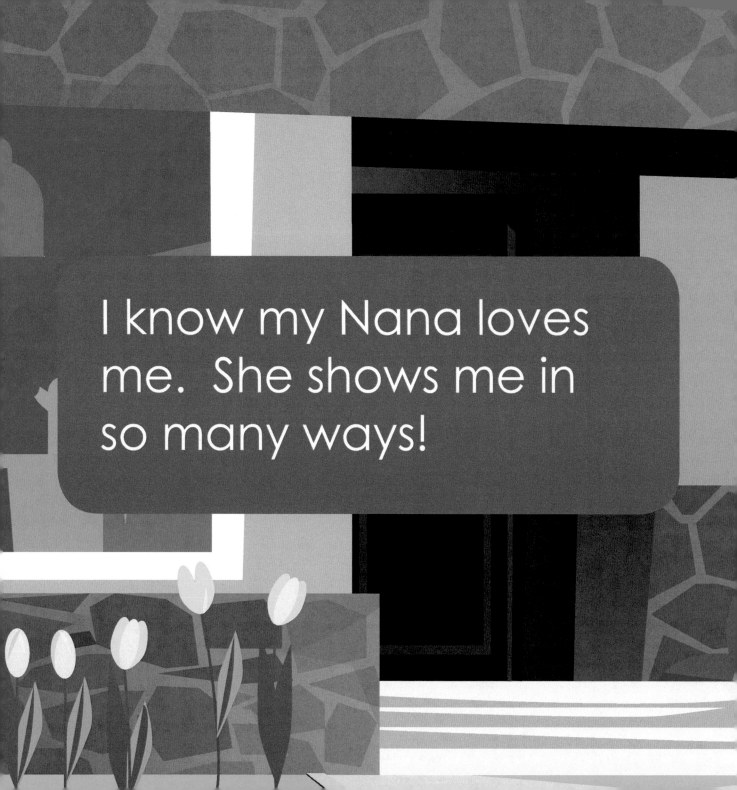

I know my Nana loves me. She shows me in so many ways!

She helps me brush my teeth. She wants me to be healthy!

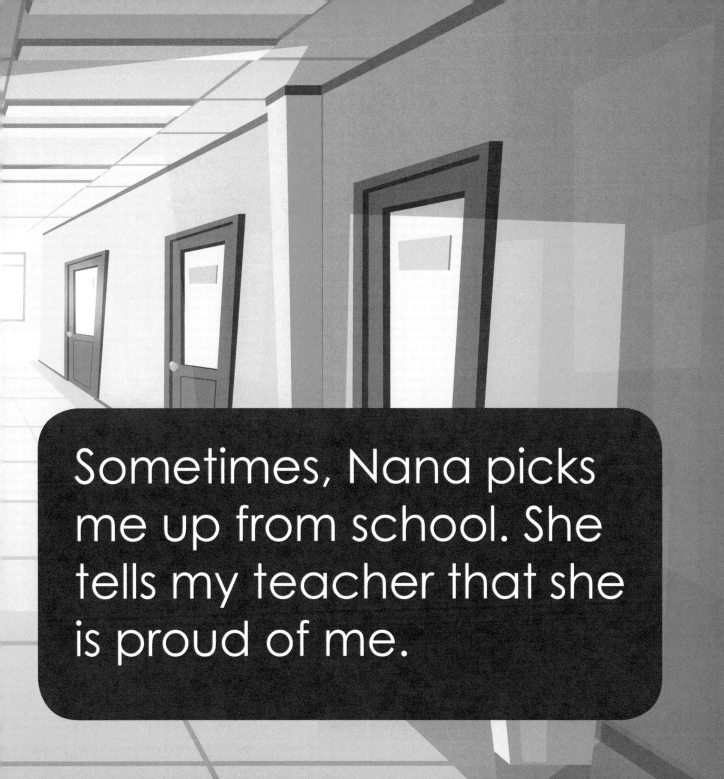

Sometimes, Nana picks me up from school. She tells my teacher that she is proud of me.

Nana likes to take me grocery shopping. (And sometimes, I get a treat.)

Nana and I feed ducks in the park.

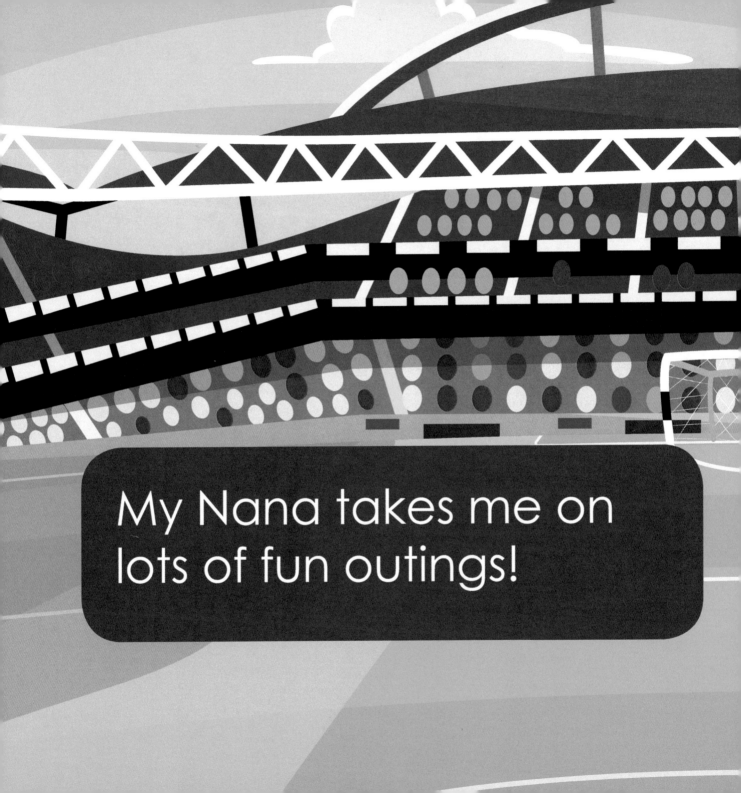

My Nana takes me on lots of fun outings!

Nana likes to take me to the playground to play.

When it is autumn, we go look at the pretty leaves together.

Even when Nana is very busy, she makes time to talk to me.

In winter, she makes sure that I am bundled up warmly.

At Christmastime, we look at the twinkling lights together.

And when I am far away, I know that my Nana thinks about me and misses me.

Made in the USA
Monee, IL
11 March 2021